I0556567

Praise for Unwilling

"I've been a huge Gerri Leen fan for years now; her work consistently blows me away. With her latest poetry collection, *Unwilling*, she does it again, weaving her gorgeous and lyrical spell that takes hold of you and never lets you go. With every poem, she draws you into a tale that's by turns bewitching, beautiful, and brutal. There's no one out there writing like Gerri Leen today. Pick up this collection immediately and prepare to be captivated."

—Gwendolyn Kiste, Lambda Literary and Bram Stoker Award-winning author of *Reluctant Immortals* and *The Haunting of Velkwood*

"*Unwilling: Poems of Horror and Darkness* takes readers to the shadowlands where angels and crows have more in common than one might expect. Gerri Leen reveals enchantment in everyday items, as she contemplates the truth hidden beneath the mask of the familiar. The grim poems in *Unwilling* are steeped in melancholy and sugared with more than a little rage. Dark feminism at its best."

—Carina Bissett, award-winning editor of *Shadow Atlas: Dark Landscapes of the Americas*

"Gerri Leen spins her poems with exquisite threads of darkness, presented in three sections. There's the mirror that holds a face, not a reflection, or about being at war with angels, joined by crows. A bar in the old west, out of time; roasted hellhounds, bringing a witch to heel, and a love song turned into a scream, all among the many mesmerizing poems in this fine collection."

—Marge Simon, Bram Stoker Award-winning poet

"From haunted household objects like mirrors and teacups to unholy alliances between humans and birds in an ongoing apocalypse, *Unwilling* is aptly titled and roils with lyrical, unearthly delights."

—AJ Odasso, author of *The Sting of It* and *The Pursued and the Pursuing*

"*Unwilling* unwinds itself to the willing reader, asking questions about humanity, divinity, and more. What answers these poems give are usually unsettling ones—when they give answers at all. Gerri Leen is at her best in this collection, thrusting the responsibility of finding answers on the reader themselves, opening doors to worlds of imagination that are eerie, and which demand that the reader stand up and engage with them as an equal. Leen's imagination is vivid and intense, and her words are unsparing. Be prepared for a long and wonderful ride with her; indeed, pack a lunch."

—Deborah L. Davitt, author of *Bounded by Eternity*

"Step into the shadowed realm of *Unwilling: Poems of Horror and Darkness*, where the echoes of classic horror tropes resonate with a haunting fresh resonance. Within these pages, poet Gerri Leen, a perennial Rhysling Award nominee whose verse has graced my own speculative anthology *Eccentric Orbits* for years, invites readers to traverse landscapes both eerie and alluring.

In the first section "Caught up in Darkness," Leen explores the depths of human fear and vulnerability, weaving lyrical tapestries that ensnare the imagination. "Monstrous Things" delves into the realms of the unknown, offering glimpses into the darkness of the human psyche. And in "Love is Hell," the poet masterfully intertwines themes of passion and torment, crafting verse that is both chilling and achingly beautiful. With a style that is as lyrical as it is unique, this collection promises to captivate lovers of both horror and literary poetry alike, offering a fresh perspective on the age-old shadows that haunt the human soul."

—Poet Laureate Emerita Wendy Van Camp

Unwilling

Poems of Horror and Darkness

By Gerri Leen

With an introduction by Rebecca Buchanan

Copyright 2024 by Gerri Leen
All Rights Reserved
ISBN: 979-8-9902007-1-5

Cover designer: SelfPubBookCovers.com/mad-moth

Dedication

With many thanks to Deborah L. Davitt, who helped this book become its best self and me a better twister of verse.

And to all the editors who have published my work,
the fellow poets who have helped me grow,
and the readers who have supported my work.

And to my Aunt Lil, who read me poetry when I was young.

Table of Contents

Introduction

Ravens and crows. Death and magic. Darkness. Power. Faith and war.

The themes that permeate Gerri Leen's poetry are many and varied, but they present a unified whole—a skeptical, questioning wonder, a wandering down serpentine paths and often off the paths; a curiosity about the world and the powers that make it, both human and other. The world is beautiful, and that beauty can inspire both awe and dread, often simultaneously. The world is dark, a darkness that can be terrible and hungry, or warm and welcoming. The world is magical, and that magic is both strange and loving, harsh and destructive. When death comes—for an individual, for a culture, for the whole wide world—it is relentless and inescapable and inevitable, and sometimes, if death likes you, she will invite you in for tea.

Leen's poetry reminds us that the world is a haunting and haunted place. Be curious. Wonder. Wander those serpentine paths—and watch your step.

—Rebecca Buchanan, Rhysling Award-winning poet and author of *Not a Princess, But (Yes) There Was a Pea, and Other Fairy Tales to Foment Revolution*

Caught up in Darkness

Unwilling

Roiling around the sorceress
The ravens carry her messages
Dodging as they gather
Avoiding the razor wire
Of her blood-red tresses
The magnetic pull of
Her abyss-black gown

She summons without
Caring what she interrupts
They have chicks in the nest
Ripe to be taken down
By hawks, shouldered
Or tailed with the same
Burning scarlet as her hair

They croak their concern
And feel her magic grip
Like needled fingers
Clawing around their throats
Dampening any resistance

Their croaks turn to silence
Except for the rush of
Wings and the mind-swept
Scream of their jailer
As one of them
Abandons all reason and
Attacks her only to dissolve
In flame and ash

The rest fly, wings
Sore from too many

Of these errands
Beating harder than
Is safe—anything
To get away from her

They see hawks
Circling their homes
They hold their cries in and
Pray to the corvid gods
That their young have
Learned to be silent
To keep their eyes closed
To not move, not even
Breathe too vigorously

For hawks see all
Not unlike the ravens' mistress
Who even now screams
For them to hurry
For there is more to do
Her cry as haunting
As a hawk's and
Twice as terrifying

What If It Hurts?

I always thought magic would feel good
Bubbly and warm, moving through
My system like a sweet wine
But it stings, sharp little jabs
At first, anyway
Then it's worse, it's agony
Necrotizing my impulses
My integrity
Until I send it out
Until I use it

Oh, hell, let's be honest: until I
Kill someone

I didn't want to
Please know that I never, ever
Wanted to hurt anyone
And it's not my fault
I didn't seek the magic out
It found me, no different than
A cold or the flu
Or Ebola, a sinister, enchanted
Hemorrhage, wearing away
My resistance

I just wanted to talk to her, that sorceress
I never wanted her power

But she died while I was there and magic
Can't perish, can't just be culled
It jumps hosts, it mutates as
It finds a new home
Taking hold, wearing down
I tried to fight it, but there's no

Cure, no vaccine, no supportive
Therapy for someone like me

So I'll give you a choice that old witch
Never gave me

Let me kill you so I can
Make this pain go away for a while
Or I'll kill myself and it will jump to you
The door's locked
You can't run away from this
Which will it be?
Annihilation or infection?
I imagine death hurts worse
But ends more quickly

Don't worry: I can wait while you decide which one of us
Will be eradicated

Mirror, Mirror

You once compared my eyes
To the sea on a stormy day
I'd like to check if they're still like that
But my mirror isn't itself right now
You know the one
We got it at that antique shop
Near the ocean the day
We drove out just for the
Hell of it, before we decided
To spend our time making
Each other miserable
The frame was so beautiful
I was mesmerized by it
To the point where I could
Ignore my own reflection
But you stopped me and held
My head between your hands
So gently, because back then you
Still loved me, and had me look
Really look, into my own eyes

That was a mistake
I knew it, the mirror knew it
Hell, even the old shopkeeper
Got up and came toward us with
A shocked "That might not be a good idea"
You were the only one who didn't
Have any idea how much of me went
Into the mirror and how much of it
Went into me
It's how I know, without looking
That it's never settled in
Never stopped thinking about its old home
Near the water—it would

Belch the ocean out at me
If it could find a way
It misses the old shopkeeper
And he cried when we bought it
But what could he do?
It was part of me and it wasn't
As if he could have me stay with him
Or that I'd want to

I think I lost you that day
When the part of me that could forgive
That could tolerate
Disappeared into silvered glass
I started to hate you
Or maybe the mirror did
It was your hands, after all,
That held me fast as the
Mirror and I first made contact
And it was like you, only
I didn't know it then
To force things
As if you were the only one who'd
Ever thought my gray eyes unique
Or unsettling
As if only you could show me how
Special I was
So special I left you when your
Games got to be too much
When I finally realized control to
You is spelled L-O-V-E

I go to the mirror and can feel the sea breeze
As I stand before it, can see
The waves crashing against the shore
I touch the beautiful frame that first drew me in

Whisper, "I'll take you home"
The mirror clears and I see myself, finally
Older and haggard but with eyes still stormy
As I lift it off the hook you put in the wall
Some special kind to hold the weight
Too bad the bulk of it was inside me, not hanging

I put it in my car and drive and drive
Because I've moved farther away from the shore
The shopkeeper is standing at the doorway
It's been ten years but he hasn't aged
And the store still looks nice even though
The rest of the area is seedy
"It wants to come home"
The old man doesn't seem surprised
"So do I"—somehow this whispered
Truth I didn't realize was mine escapes
The mirror and I have absorbed so much of
Each other, neither of us given a choice in this
Am I even me anymore?

He takes the mirror and strokes it
Lovingly, speaking to it in a language
I can't begin to understand
Or even describe
Then he flings it to the ground
I tense but while the gorgeous frame
Splinters, the glass doesn't even scratch
"I always try to break it first" he says with
Remorse that seems genuine
Even as he reaches for my head
The same way you did
When you first introduced me to
This cursed looking-glass
The part of me that's still in the mirror

Watches the old man break my neck
With the same sincere regret
"Goodbye," the mirror whispers
Just before everything goes dark

Where the Light Ends

Go toward the light
They say, with certainty

Not knowing that the light
Starts the tunnel
But doesn't finish it
Where do I go now?

I've fallen halfway
And it's colder at the end
I can feel the draft from here
And me in my sister's dress

Her favorite, "Don't take it"
She said, she always said

Why did I take it?
Everyone knows it
Including the guy who hit me
Speaking her name, not kindly

Boom and boom and down
This tunnel, this crosshatched
Terrifying cylinder of . . . what?
I am undone and yet

And yet

The light is warm
Maybe I'll just stay here

The Devil's Champion

You said no hand but mine could end this life
You said I was too bright to have to kneel
You did not say how hard would be this strife

My anger when they said I'd be his wife
Led me to make this unexpected deal
You said no hand but mine could end this life

'Twas better to wage war than be his wife
Your words were made to tantalize and heal
You did not say how hard would be this strife

I never knew this world could be so rife
With conflict and with power some would steal
You said no hand but mine could end this life

For years I've been your warrior not a wife
So long that very little else feels real
You did not say how hard would be this strife

And now I sit and play here with this knife
It's time to make a wound that cannot heal
You said no hand but mine could end this life
You did not say how hard would be this strife

The Corvid-Human Alliance

I motion the crows out, two by two, keeping their
Youngsters back with me because it's the bargain

We've made with the group, if they fight for us in the air
We'll keep their children safe from the angels on the ground

Crows will mob an eagle or a hawk
Angels, as it turns out, are just sacred raptors

Guarding no one and nothing except their piece of the sky
Grounding planes and confusing targeting systems

With EMP bursts from golden trumpets
The few missiles that do break through are brought

Down by their fiery swords
Nothing made by man can touch them

They taunt us with this fact, choirs of them
Singing of invulnerability, using wing-wind to magnify the
sound

But crows aren't made by man but by the god these
Monsters serve, and corvids fully embrace the concept

That the enemy of my enemy is my ally
Not that the angels are targeting birds

But their fire falls indiscriminately, burning habitats
In a way that makes humans look like destruction amateurs

The resulting ash clogs streams, fills nests, ruins rookeries
Coats feathers, suffocates young birds and the wise crones of
the group

I've cleaned off so many birds, watching ashy grey give way to
Rainbow black, the sheen of oil playing out over feathers I'd

Previously touched only when shed and left on the ground
But now I've grown used to the feel of a beak on my skin

Patient or not, gentle or not, battle by battle
We are learning to speak crow the same way we

Learned to speak cat or dog or horse
By movements, by vocalizations, by attitude

I hear a scream above me, corvid and angelic both
And black and white wings are wrapped in a

Peregine-fast plunge to earth, more crows following
Some on fire and I call the water teams over

The crows still whole are pecking, going for eyes and the base
Of the wings where angels seem to bleed the most easily

The angel is stunned and one of our warriors kicks the fire-sword
Out of the way and stabs the angel with a hearty branch

Scavenged with care, any manmade enhancements make sticks useless
We are becoming adept at searching nature for death

Behind the fence that divides our compound from others
There is a line of the faithful, wailing as the angel dies

They kneel and chant that we will be damned
A few pray that we will be saved, that we will see the angels

As they do—a sign of the long-awaited end times, the harbingers
Of the glory of their religion, of the glory of apocalypse

We see nothing but how we must once have appeared
To the rest of nature, before the angels took our place as apex predator

Winged killers that fly high and care not at all that we
Were once beloved of their god and their charges to look after

Creatures so sick of their place in the natural order
That they rebelled, fled Heaven, and waged war on us

Or maybe it really was on the orders of their maker
Maybe this is how it all ends, in fire and ash and the taunts

Of supernatural beings we thought looked out for us
Or at least didn't bear us any ill will, not like demons were supposed to

Demons haven't appeared, no horns or claws or stench of sulphur
Although if they fought with us, we'd probably take their help

How long can we and our black-winged allies hold out?
I hear the caw that means attack, I look up and see a new foe

Being mobbed and I grab the branch I have killed more angels than
I can count with and wait for the crows to bring this next one down

The prayers from the fence get louder, someone yells that I'm
a lost soul
But overhead, crows scream louder and angelic blood drips
down

And I don't feel lost, I don't feel forsaken
I catch a smoldering bird and dunk it in a water bucket before

It can burn too much and it hops onto my shoulder, gently
Creaking as it nips my cheek in thanks, then it's off again

There is a clatter behind me, a child has gathered branches
Stout things that should be beyond her ability to carry

But we're so much stronger than we once thought
She refills buckets and watches the sky, another pair of eyes

A juvenile crow hops onto her shoulder and I see the future
Superimposed on this present and it shines in multicolor hues

Buried in raven black—if we can hold the line, might there be
a
World where bird and man move together, discovering
victory

In their unexpected unity? An alliance that took on the
messengers
Of a god and persevered when all seemed well and truly lost

A Jaunty Tune

The train left me, the conductor
Said not to wander too far
But I never thought they'd go
Leaving me here in this empty
Wreck of a town

This isn't a real stop, just an
Area where my tourist train
Could pull off to make way for freight
This ghost town gives and receives
No passengers

I wanted to stretch my legs
I can't say why I went so far
Does it make sense if I thought
This old saloon looked inviting
In the afternoon heat?

But it's not; it's cobwebbed and dusty
Although they must have tours here
The player piano is tinkling
Out of tune, but maybe activated
When I walked in?

I can almost smell filthy cotton, wet leather
And wool, the sound of taffeta and lace
Hear the straight pour from a whiskey bottle
The loud pop of bullets ricocheting
The music goes on

I wonder how long before the train
Passes back this way? Can I flag it down?
How long is that piano going to go?

Surely it's on a battery timer because
I see no power source

The place goes cold, and I hear
Playing cards being laid down, dancing
Feet clomping, and a straight razor being sharpened
I back away, toward the door, the cold increases
The door won't open

The piano changes tune suddenly
The plinking of keys now mournful
I look for a roll, the thing that makes
A player piano play by itself
There isn't one

Someone Comes Knocking

My uncle told me
Sometimes a knock
Means someone must die
He sat near the fire
In our cabin by the water
His back to the rest of the room
On a night when the moon was black
And wind whistled through old windows

Days later the attic echoed him
As below my feet
A knock sounded
I didn't scare easily
But I hid under
One of the beds
Felt spiders skitter on my skin
Less scary than whatever was at the door

I stayed there until the
Crunch of tires on gravel
Meant my parents were home
They found a card in the door
Announcing a new church
Stupid to have been scared
A week later, an arrest in our
Tiny town—a predator using God as introduction
My uncle's superstition had saved me

My new house is spider free
My uncle long dead, the old cabin sold
But the moon goes black
As wind screeches through the windows
A knock sounds at the door and
I want to hide but can't think where

This house has no attic
The door opens on its own
Young wood creaking impossibly

I see no one, but a voice says
The first time's just a warning

Enrichment Items

I placed the moon for you
Still dripping, at the top of your container
Wounded regolith oozing under my fingernails
Reflected light illuminating your space
No sun, but it was reflecting off you
My treasure
My love

My prisoner

Here, have a tree
Black and tired
See as your new moon lights up its branches
Perhaps it will leaf out
Despite the harsh way I pulled
It from the ground it rested in over winter
I found you in winter too
Plants don't do well with me
If it dies, I'll find another
I'd do anything for you

Except let you go

Topiary

Welcome to my forest
A fabulous place
Green and lush, dripping with
Before-sunrise dew, and sometimes the
Flood of a late-night storm

Ignore that it lies in the middle of a desert

Marvel at the trees
Pruned in such a way to mimic life
There: a tiger, a mounted warrior, a jackal
And yes, they each have their own perfume
Wafting in the night air

Ignore that it's always night here

See flowers that grow in almost-spatters
Around the oh-so-realistic trees
Some bright red, others almost rusty
They have a copper-penny scent
It is not unpleasant

Ignore that they look like blood

I will have you stand here
Where there is a gap between
The tiger and the warrior
A prince is just the thing to add
Your flowers are a particularly rich scarlet

Ignore how long it takes to bleed them out

Good and Faithful Servant

As I stand behind her, unable to look at
Her face, she reaches back and takes my
Chapped and swollen hand in her youthful one

You've borne witness
You've moved energy when it was stalled
You've dealt doom and are yet
Innocent in the dealing

I take in the sea, dead and airless
The land burnt or buried under dank water
The bodies floating—I never wanted this

You asked for none of this
The task is punishment for
A moment of neglect so far in the past I forget
Why I was so angry with you

I've always understood energy
I've always dreamed of her wrath
I've always known I'm not simply human

And yet you've embraced the darkness
You were born a creature of light and yet
Destruction and chaos called you
Truly you are my child

I feel the truth of her words in my soul
There's no panic as I take in the wreckage
Only regret that I couldn't save those I love

It's an irony: I made you human so you would feel
And now that's all you do, such noble emotions

From such a dark thing as you
Are those tears I see on your face?

They are but I swipe them away viciously
She's never happy, not when I worked to save people
And not now, when I worked her later will: this darkness

If I were to ask you your deepest wish, what would it be?
To hear your lost lover's voice again, one last time?
To rest once more in the embrace of your human mother?
Or perhaps to be the child who had no idea what's to come?

I don't answer; I don't have to
She knows me far too well
Knows exactly where to push the hardest

I can't decide if it would be more fun to rebuild this world
Or create another? What? You thought you were finished?
The mere fact you thought you might be
Shows you are not

Her logic is obscene and I fall to my knees and squeeze
scorched
Earth through my fingers—but it's too late
She's already starting, remaking destruction into a pristine
home

You'll be one of the first to be born on this latest Earth
But until it's time for humans to repopulate my world
I'll keep you with me—I do enjoy our quiet moments
Don't you?

Bone China

"Have some tea," Santa Muerte says
As she sweetens her cup
With a lollipop made of honey
She has no milk or lemon
No fancy rock sugar
"It's Darjeeling, autumn flush"
Because she likes it strong
Substantial in the mouth
Lingering in the finish
No evanescent spring flush for her
Or a somewhere-in-between summer flush

She hands me a cup with a bug
Printed on it (but no bugs in it
Because I check—one never knows
With her) and fills it from a
Clay teapot, the expensive kind
From Taiwan, and she smiles
As she sees me studying it
"I get around—did you think
I only stay in Mexico?"

And yes, I did think that
But I don't want to admit it
So I blow on the tea to cool it
And the odors of muscatel
Of stone fruits and the lovely basic
Tea smell of camellia sinensis
Waft back at me
"Honey?" she asks, holding out her
Lollipop with a smile that says she's
Well aware I don't like honey
Except on cornbread or biscuits

She puts it back on her saucer
With a wink

She waits, her appearance sliding from
Skeletal to flayed, her mouth open
As stars fly into it
"Ix Chel is more your speed," she says
So casually, as if she's fine that my loyalty
Might be to a gentler goddess from
Another pantheon
"Mictecacihuatl frightens many"
But she's taken on more than
Simply watching bones
She's universal, not just Aztec
She takes souls now, grants favors
And apparently is quite the tea fan

She laughs, "You amuse me
I'm so glad you're dead"
I take a sip of her tea
It's delicious and as I swallow
I feel my body dissolving
The skin peeling off
As a conch sounds, as a jaguar
Screams, as a serpent hisses
It hurts, for a moment, but only
For a moment
"More tea?" she asks
I hold out my cup
With a skeletal hand
And enjoy teatime
In the home of the dead

Release Me

Mist dips and twists around me
Reducing the visible world to the length of my arm
My sword drips red into this world of grey
I hear the paper-rasp of snakeskin under my feet
The whine of a dog somewhere to my side
I must get to the exact center
Where two straight paths cross
I cannot feel him yet
But his voice, his sweet voice
There, just . . . over . . . there

He died at the crossroads
His soul is Hers, but his heart belongs to me
I ignore the confusion of the center
Reach behind me and it's summer
Forward and winter's chill is met
Beloved, I am here
Which of us whispers that?
His spirit or my flesh?
I close my eyes and feel the press of lips

This isn't my land anymore
The conquerors fight harder each year
To hold it as their own
But I have to come
On this day, at this time
When walls fall and realms merge
So I wait, kneeling, sword on the ground
Feeling his ghostly touches
Praying to this dark goddess that my enemies
Will find me—and end this

She made a deal with me
To join my love, I must die here too

But I cannot strike the blow myself
And it's getting harder to make the journey
Harder to fight my way through to this spot
This quest is her joke, just ask the poor dog
Abandoned and left to rot
The snake, flayed before it was ready to shed
And me, the besotted warrior
Cajoling the old one for my lover
When she could grant him to me with a wave
I can hear her laughter
It sounds like wolfsong, so eerie and raw
I know no one will come to end my misery

I wait anyway

I See You

In the ruins of a temple
Your jaguar pelt is as shiny
As the first time we met here
How many centuries ago was it?
I forget but I imagine
You do not

I wore Macaw feathers and held
A stingray barb and you
Were dragged onto the ball field
Because my husband thought
If sacrificing our enemies
And our children
Couldn't save us
Maybe you could

They expected you to do something
Spectacular, godlike
Instead, you killed them all
You're no ordinary jaguar
But I was no ordinary queen
And your bite didn't kill me
Even if it took years for the scars to fade

No, don't run
I'm not here for revenge
Our time was over then
And it may be again
Sit with me and sing the songs
Of Xibalba as I remember what this place
Was like when it was filled with life
And hope and blood
Always so much blood

Your fur is soft
Last time I touched you was to
Throw you off me
Now we can sit like this
On the steps of the temple
The moon bright on us, the tourists—
What few of them remain—gone
As we listen to the songs
Of the jungle night
Together

Caught You

Remember the nights this subway stop
Sat empty, a playground for us
And our stupid games of hide
And seek? Remember how
I would laugh at you
In your preppy
Jacket and
Khaki
Pants?

I'm not laughing anymore, am I?
Even though you still want to play
You look at me like years and
Death haven't robbed us of
The joy of this place
You start to count
And I laugh
Like old
Times

I'll just pretend that you never jumped
And doomed yourself to haunt this spot
So happy to see me, not
Even knowing you're dead
Until someone does
The simple spell
To let you
Leave this
Place

I let you hide first, almost lose you
As you slide through rather than go
Around things but of course I
Do eventually

Find you; you find me
Much more quickly
But that just
Seems fair
Right?

I'm tired when we stop but you're not
Even breathing hard, and your eyes
Sparkle just like they used to
You seem to be at peace
I say I love you
As I pull out
The spell and
Set you
Free

Housemates

The house sang to you
Its listing on the MLS
Carefully making strengths out of
Eccentricities
You'd seen so many other houses
Known as soon as you crossed the threshold
They weren't "it"
You stepped into this one
And felt at peace
Would you have moved on
If you'd realized
Peace can be the absence of all kinds of things
Not just chaos

Your health had never been great
You didn't notice the house
Beginning to suck you dry
You felt safe inside it, even if you
Also felt horrible
Tired turned to exhausted
Small headaches turned to much worse
"Maybe it's the house," worried friends said
Thinking radon or mold or some other issue
Certainly not the truth
Was it you or the house that answered
"No, the house is perfect"?

It seems to have stopped
Tugging so hard at you
You hover closer to life than death
But not fully in either
Housebound and hearing finally
The voices of those who came before
"Welcome" was what you heard that

First zen day in the house
"Run" was what the others actually said
Spirit-to-carnal translators are tricky
Until you're halfway there

Now they entertain you
"It's a beautiful view," the one called Maude says
"I've always loved the squirrels"
You think you should feed the squirrels
While you can still make it out of the door
The familiar lethargy takes over
Tomorrow, the house says
Tomorrow you can go to the bird store
Pick up seeds and a birdbath, too

It will let you out so you have
Amusements in the yard and no reason to leave
The house picks at your soul
Maude points at a fox
Upstairs you hear the others arguing
Over which room you'll get
Once you're dead
You close your eyes and nap
The house steals your dreams

Monstrous Things

Amateurs

You poor sweet fools
Did you think I wouldn't
Notice your traps?
Lethal little spike-balls
Collapsing walkways
Tripwires and the smell of
Black powder permeating
Everything—who do you`
Think you're dealing with?
And why aren't you running
Instead of putting up
This laughable resistance?
Put down your weapons
Listen to me because you seem
To be missing some vital information
I could crush you like a
Bug, but I'm not what's
Coming, in fact I'm running
Too—let that sink in
A destroyer like me: afraid
Now abandon those toys
And flee while there's still time
But run fast because it's hungry
And if you look appetizing
To me, imagine how tasty
You'll seem to it

I Remember This Place

You sought me
Down long fields of rotting corn
Through rivers red with blood
You came
Armed with weapons
Forged by monks
All for me
Another champion in my way
Shining with purity
Be gone
You shouted as you drew your sword
You aimed for my neck—poor choice
Horn is hard
And dragon scale even harder
And I adorn myself with both
You ran
When your sword broke in two
When your dagger bounced off
I chased
Back through the river
Down through the corn
You fell
I did what you could not
Removed your head from your neck
Your skull
Is just one of many I carry with me
Unremarkable in every way
Except here
I pull it out to try to recall your face
Then drop it where your body fell
So long ago

Fetch

Breathing slowly, carefully
Trying not to notice anyone
Or anything for too long
Lest they strike, eager as puppies
After a stick or the ball or a
Head, they brought me a head
Baby demons imprint, you see
And they come in litters
Someone really should say that
Before they sell you a conjuring kit

Swamp Glow

You created a home for me in this swamp
Green light glows from putrefying logs
A kettle over a fire holds jambalaya
Made of broken dreams and lost chances
You bid me climb stairs zigzagging crazily
Carrying me far from sucking ground while
Magic holds this structure up and the same
Power shines from the windows

You think I can't tell those holes
Are eyes, not glass?
Silly mortal

Loas come in many guises and I've worn the
Façade of an ingénue so long
My seams are invisible
You never guessed what I was
I've always known what you were
You urge me to climb but I stop
To pick some red mushrooms
Their spongy form soft against my hands

Flesh of my flesh
Poison of my poison
Beautiful additions to this meal you've made

I drop them into the kettle
The green haze intensifies making
The windows glow: they can feel what I am
"Welcome," they seem to say and
The jambalaya begins to bubble
I peel a piece of mushroom
From the side of the kettle and chew

My flesh doesn't burn
From where I touched the iron
My tongue doesn't swell

I see you finally understand as I don't
React to the toxin, as I smile—my lips
Perhaps tinted crimson from the fungus
You realize with a visible swallow that you'll
Be the only one going up those stairs
Unless, of course, you prefer a last meal
You can share the jambalaya with me
It really looks quite delicious

The Stairs

What lies at the bottom
Of the stairs?
(Don't go down there
You'll never come back up)
The cellar—what makes something
A cellar and not a basement?
Other than it's a creepier name?
The bricks glow, clean and bright
The staircase looks strong
Beautiful barn wood, reclaimed
Probably from nearby
What lies at the bottom
Of the stairs?

What lies at the top
Of the stairs?
(Don't venture up there
You'll never come home)
Light shines from under the door
Or when the door squeals open
And we run and hide
I sometimes see a figure
Aglow with light, and the bricks
Are beautiful and strange
What lies at the top
Of the stairs?

Blood of My Blood

I created you, beautiful creature
From need and loneliness—and magic

I didn't even know I had until
You stood there, fully formed

Allowing me to finally see how
I must look to others once the

Mirror is abandoned and all
Angles are accessible

Blood calls to blood and so you
Never stray too far from me

Even if I wish you would
Even if I've tried to make you

I've dropped you off in the
Middle of nowhere and sang

Endless nonsense songs just in
Case you can echolocate off my thoughts

And for the time we're apart, I can
Breathe again, can feel myself healing

Becoming whole without you
My shadow twin, sucking the life out of me

But you find me, no matter how far
Or which direction I go

And you never come back clean
There's blood under your nails

And flesh between your teeth
And I haven't the heart to ask

Why and how many and did you
Enjoy it or was it just the way you

Survive when I'm not there to give you
Some of my life force to sustain you

You leech, you vampire—only not really
Because vamps can be put down

A simple stake, some garlic, a trip
To a church for holy water

And my problem would be taken care of
But you're never taken care of

You're invulnerable or so it seems
Because I once stabbed you as you slept

And you pulled the knife out and bled
For a day or two all over the rental house

Until I fled again and you chased
And that was yet another damage deposit

I'll never get back because of you
And I don't even know what you are

Other than a better mirror than the ones that
Hang in whatever place I am calling home

I am aging—too fast—as you suck the life from me
You're aging too so maybe if I die, you'll follow

And if I were a better person, I'd take the chance
Of being wrong and put an end to myself

But I'm not or I'd have never made you
Never run from you knowing each time

What you do to survive until you find me again
I'd never let you back in, hating myself for

Feeling sorry for you, for not being able
To say no to myself—or to this truer version of me

You love me—you never punish me when you return
Always look at me with hurt eyes and a

Quivering lip, always sink into my arms and
Make me promise to never, ever leave you again

And I do. Each time, I do—does that make me kind
Or more cruel than you could ever be?

All Alone in God's House

You remember riding past the church
Its red, red windows
A stained-glass rose
Lighting up the dark
A safe place to run to

Your dad laughed at that idea
"Don't go into God's house
'Less you're clean of sin"
"Or what?" you asked
He never did say

You're running now, in trouble
The church is dark
Sirens sound behind you
You open the door
Breathe in cold air

You step in, heart racing
Hair inching up your neck
Nothing clean about you—
And it's too late
To wipe your soul at the door

You hear shuffling, smell something burning
From high up, red eyes shine
Like a stained-glass rose
You realize too late
The windows have always been clear

Medusa Ups Her Game

Snakes for hair is so last year
Give me webbing, not spider-made
But of computer linkages
Turn you to stone?
Very old school—let me work
More subtly this time
As I weave my way into your
Social network, as I curate
Your feeds to bring you the
Things you fear most, the things
You hate most, the things you'll
Do anything to stop, to own, to destroy
Perseus should have left me alone
I've abandoned stone for fire
And this time you can watch
As I burn it all down
You'll long for snakes when this is done

They Call

They call me mad
But I see the way
Your visage slips
And slides as if
You're only partially
Connected to this plane

They call me paranoid
But I see your even
Features—those gentle
Eyes—transform into
Something far less
Benign than you let on

They call me cursed
But I cannot accept
You as our new hope
Cannot kneel at your
Feet and beg for grace
It's not in you to bestow

They call me evil
But we're two of a kind
And I can see the
Spark of malignance
Shining through your
Message of peace

They call me Cassandra
Now that it's too late and
You've sucked this world
Dry and left them alone in
The temples they set
Up in your honor

They can call me
Whatever they like
But will they listen
Any better when
The next you
Comes along?

Pick a Card

You have drawn the high priestess
In my deck, you can't tell which
Way she's looking
Her white gown—dingy if you study it
Sufficiently—flows around her in such
A way as to obscure which is front, which back
The arms of the gown long and uneven
The train extending both forward and back
How does she walk?
(Does she walk?)
Or does she just stare into the black mirror
Behind (ahead of) her?
Does she see your future or is she holding it
Back, to save you, to spare you?
Would she do that? She doesn't know you
Or does she? Is she saying hello?
Or is that simply her stomach rumbling?

Yes, those are leaves, gathered at the edges
Of the gown, not green though, brittle and rusty
They shiver as she breathes, sighs, murmurs
Words you cannot hope to understand
Ask your question while she is ready
To talk with you, if you have the courage
For she will answer truthfully
And truth often hurts

You want another card?
Apologies, but this is what you drew
Ask your question, but frame it as if you know
Whether she looks at you or away
Because it will matter
Yes, just one question
No, there's no one else waiting for a reading

Yes, it is getting darker in here
I suggest you hurry: she devours questions
But failing that: you're a nice second choice
For a meal, and it's been a bit
Since anyone's drawn her
So she's ravenous

Lost Dogs

Have you seen my dogs?
They're large and black
Imposing and know no master
Only me, their mistress
Perhaps dog is the wrong word
Hellhounds is more accurate
Rough and ready and loyal to a fault
I sent them out and they
Haven't come back
I can't remember
The last time that was so
They can't be killed I was told
When the one who made me
Gave me these two
To keep me company
I see by your eyes that you
Know they're not immortal
Not impermeable to certain types
Of weapons, like the one hanging
From your waist that stinks of
Magic and hatred

Is that their scent, I smell on
Your jacket of black leather
Recently tanned?
Is that their flesh turning
On the spit over your fire?
Is that your woman, stringing
Tendon-strong thread into her needles?
I found the dogs, you see
I found their bones
How did you leave them so perfectly intact?
Was it so I'd know?

Was it so I'd come?
Was it so you could kill me too?
Some might say those mutts
Were the best part of me
So perhaps you've already done that

I'll tell you a secret
They weren't my pets but my
Jailers, great canine guards charged
With monitoring me
When the one who made me
Grew weary of watching me every
Second of every day
And sent me out, with a hellhound
On either side, never leaving me, never
Ever giving me a moment's peace
Oh, I'd slip away but they'd always find me
Quickly and with harsh fangs
See these scars?
But this time, they didn't sniff me out
You've changed everything

I should let you live in gratitude
But I don't know how long I have
Before my maker sends out more hounds
They may already be on the hunt
I need to make the most of my freedom
And I'm dreadfully hungry
And while I'm sure roasted hellhound
Is a delicacy where you're from
I prefer my meat to walk on two legs, not four
Your sword won't help you, but give it a try
Maybe you can end this
Put me down the way you did those beasts
Come on, it's been an eternity since I had a

Good fight—or a bad one
And really, someone should avenge
My poor dead pups

String Theory

It gets loose
In the night
That damned puppet
I can hear it
Clickity-clack
Running up, sliding down
It trips sometimes
Tangles up its strings
Takes me days to work them free

Even longer to clean up the blood

I should tell
Maybe a priest
Could exorcise it
Sprinkle it
Salt it
Make it stop getting loose
Let me sleep
Just one night
All the way through

Without having to clean up the mess

But maybe not
He'd wonder why
I never said a word before
How many dead?
I never told
I never tried to make it stop
And if I did
Would it stop?
Or would it come after me?

And who would clean up then?

Love is Hell

Spring, When I Met You (Spring, When I Woke)

I woke, melting ice my welcome
Back to this world
My skin danced around me
Dusty as an old snakeskin
And I shuddered under the snow
And shook and scratched
Until I could feel it giving
And above my skin the cold
Was giving way as sun
Softened what I knew was my grave
I crawled out of my old skin as I
Clawed my way to the light
Your last whispers still ringing in my head

Who are you whispering to now?
Do they know what you are?

You had no idea what I was
To be fair, neither did I
But now I remember my
Grandma's words about rot
And renewal and how some people are
Like flowers that bloom only once
And others can come again the next year
But she fell down dead the summer I turned
Twelve and I never found out the truth

So I was scared when you killed me
Was it fun for you making me love and then fear you?

I remember the ripeness of the mulch just laid
Down on the beds in the park the day we met
You were walking, head down, earbuds in
And I smiled at you because you weren't looking

But you caught me anyway, the expression locked
Between us, like a rabbit held by a hawk
You were hunting me then, weren't you?
Only I didn't know it; I thought I discovered you
So handsome, the shy smile hiding the
Emptiness inside you—how dead you are inside

Dead enough to bury me here, in this same park
The mulch is even more pungent now that I'm twice alive

I'm naked and soon there may be a passerby who sees me
And I should care but I can smell bodies
There are more like me here
Well, not like me—they're only once-alives
But I can smell the decomposition
I've heard it's a unique smell and it's true
But there are variations, each one I find
Like tree-rings, like carbon dating
This one from last year, that one much older
How long have you been doing this?
And why is your scent layered on top of theirs
Over and over—you must come here so often
Had you just visited them the day we met?
The wind blows a familiar scent coming
Down the path—have I awakened on a day you visit
And won't you be surprised at what you'll find?

Snakes don't eat while they shed—like them, newly risen in a
Body that fully fits my rage, I'm hungry and you smell delicious

Slither

Her memories of love
Are shed
Like a snakeskin
Rubbed off on a rock
Drying in the sand
Too small
Itching and pulling on
Muscles that long
To slither away
To something new
Her tongue flicks out
Heat of a body
Found with a sense not shared
With mammals
You think you're sitting still
But you radiate "I'm here"
She coils, anticipating
The strike, the locking of fangs
Making you hers
Love is to the death
Yours, of course
Not hers
Eventually, she'll shed you too
Just another skin along the trail

Untitled in Porcelain

Crackled glaze on the vase
Terracotta and turquoise
With cinnabar stamping
Delicate enameled Sakura
Falling from broken branches
With black leaves, dusty
Or is it ash covering them?
Studded birds in grayscale
Sit in the wreckage
Their imagined song sweet
In the crumbling emptiness
Next to the vase is a
Card, parchment of ivory
In beautiful calligraphy
It says: My world
Since you left it
There is no signature

Leaving the Stars Behind

You sang, songs of love
Songs of passion
Songs so softly sung that I had
To pause to hear your voice

You brought the stars down
Snuggling around us like a comforter
They burned, they sizzled
And they hummed in harmony with you

Your claws hurt at first
But love made them tolerable
Ecstasy and pain mingled
As the sky descended and we rose

We melded into a black that was
Velvet and sandpaper both on my skin
Your song turned to a scream
The stars fled

You sing still
Songs of possession, loud as a siren
But bundled safe in night
I barely hear them

Final Resting Place

You seek an urn
I can tell before you even
Head to that part of my shop
And as always
I can't resist the urge to reach
For your sorrow—or lack thereof
To determine
What kind of pottery
Would suit you best
Terracotta for a lifelong love
Porcelain for a love that was yet new
Raku for a tumultuous union
Pit-fired for an arranged marriage
That somehow proved to be a love match
But no—this is no unexpected loss
The dearly departed died by your hands
I'd offer black raku
But I feel this was no crime of passion
You planned it
The same way I planned the intricate
Carvings of my chattered pieces
And there—my gift never lies
You're drawn to the gouged slip
As surely as a cat is to catnip
Fortunately for you I am but a potter
And not a detective
As I ring you up, I whisper softly
"Your secret's safe with me"

Terroir

Good sir, do you know
What makes spirits, ciders
Beers and wines unique?
Terroir: the effect of the land and the clime
Rain and sun and elevation
And things that squiggle and dig
Specific to where we are

I embrace terroir
But that cider you're enjoying
Is full of things less tangible
Blood from a cat's last kill
The hopes of a young bride
Dashed by a crow's mournful caw
The last gasps of a dying man
And the sweat of the wife who buried him

Come savor the notes of toffee and butter
And apple, of course apple
Crisp and sweet, or of a green so sour
It puckers the stomach, not just lips
But apples of other kinds too
The apple of my eye, buried here
When the doctors wouldn't come
Because they don't like what I am

Why, you're a doctor, aren't you?
You've worked this area for years
Weren't you in town the night I sent
The boy next door to fetch help?
Didn't you refuse to come?
That green-apple sour hides a world
Of poison or maybe just an herb

That paralyzes but doesn't kill
I wonder what aspect you'll bring
When I bury you next to my girl
Alive

Dark Wings

You think me fallen but I'm not
Broken, not bleeding and these wings
Not crushed but just sprouting
Circling around me as the staircase you
Pushed me down spirals from you
You think yourself above me but
It's just a matter of perspective
If you could lie here
Next to me, your own black feathers
Growing, slipping, itching as they
Create first a stole then true
Glorious wings
You might realize that I'm the one
With the better view
I can see you fully, enraged and
So afraid I'd leave you
You'd rather I ceased to exist

As I lie here, some rough magic
Wrapping me in its spell
I see the all of you, the outside and the
Inside and it's beautifully hideous
And soon I'll be nothing like you
Once my wings finish growing
Once they dry and I can fly
You will see that I have only
Up to go while you can never hope
To follow me, can never hope to do
Anything other than flee back to the home
I can't abide a moment longer
Run back to whatever you have when I'm
No longer part of your life
And sit, silent and untouched
Alone because you pushed me to a death

That laughed at you, that caught me up with
Soft hands and scouring winds
Winds that will soon carry me out of here
Winds that keep you up there, when I know
You'd like to come down and finish the job
So go, flee, before I find out what other
Dark gifts this magic has given me

We All Want to Be Mermaids When We're Young

My sweetest memories were when we swam together
While autumn danced into winter
In a town where the population quartered
After summer was over and we had the salt water
(Colder and colder as the days moved on)
To ourselves, you with your tail and the
Razor-sharp smile I always found comforting
Me with my gangly arms and legs
Trying to be as graceful as you, to not
Splash or make a sound
To hold my breath as long as I could
As inside my house
(The only one not closed for the
Winter on our end of the beach)
My parents screamed at each other
Since I wasn't around to scream at

You tried to rescue me
If I could have followed you to
The Deeps, I would have and you'd have
Welcomed it—and you'd have loved
Me more than either of my parents
Ever did, but I was weak, I was . . . human
So you taught me the next best thing
How to use an oyster shell like a knife
Which kelp made the best garottes
Which mussels were tainted and would
Sicken and lay someone low, vomiting and pale
Which fish to never eat—unless you wanted to die
Or wanted someone else to
(Just in case things got too bad)

You left before the snows came
(You move constantly, seeking fresh feeding grounds

You said it would be years before you were in
This inlet again) but before you went, you pulled
Me close and bit me, deep on the shoulder
In a way you said would mark me
So sharks and jellies and other things that might
Hurt me would recognize I was yours
Not to be messed with, a foster child of the sea
Then you dove and you didn't break the surface
But the screaming kept up in the house and your bite
Rode my skin (healing unnaturally fast) right next
To fresh bruises from my mother, deeper wounds
From my father's words—it's hell to know you
Were never wanted except by someone who
Could never have you

Close to My Heart

Your caws were my alarm clock
The sight of you on the wheelbarrow
My husband had turned into a planter
My only comfort after he died
I'd leave you food and you'd leave
Me corvid treasures: a bottlecap, one half
Of a silver earring, a gold button

One day, as I sat on the log by the water
You flew down, onto the bricks of the firepit
Your head cocked, your caws so gentle
And I realized I'd only ever seen you alone
But crows mate for life
Live in groups, at least part of the year
The idea that you'd also been left behind
Was a terrible comfort

I found you one day in the carport
A trail of blood on the gravel from the road
You were grounded, wing torn from
Some idiot target-shooting
Or maybe worse, maybe hunting
Your kind should be safe from that
You were still alive
I sat with you, unsure what to do

Before I could decide if the vet
Or the ranger at the park was the
Better option, you were gone
I've heard crows mourn their dead
But none came to sing you to wherever
Crows go when they die
So I put you in a box and googled

Taxidermist, and found a way to
Keep you with me

Your varnished skull hangs from a leather thong
Your powerful, clever beak enameled
To make it as black as the feather
Dangling next to it
I hooked you to a silver ring
The kind that would have captured
Your attention, that might have ended
Up as one of your gifts to me

Sometimes, I think I hear your caw coming
From beneath my jaw, over my heart
Where you hang, on the outside
It makes people uncomfortable
I don't care: where were they
When I was alone and
The sweet sound of your cries
And the rush of your wings
Were my only solace?

Spare the Fire, Spoil the Brute

If you don't want to know what she is
Don't ask, don't go through her things

Don't follow her to the woods and watch her
Throw off her clothes and dance skyclad

Don't feel faint from the fumes of incense
And herbs and the slightly charred scent of magic

Or is it magick? The books you've checked have it
Both ways. With a "K" or without, it doesn't matter

She's powerful, she's beautiful, and she's a
Witch, God help you, she's a witch and you're not

You can't raise the power you can feel, if only by the way
Your hair rises on your arms and the back of your neck

She's evil. That's what you'll say as you make sense of this
Even though she's never hurt you, or anyone else either

You'll stop her: you're a good boy and don't hold with such
Things as this, as bonfires in the wood, and dancing golden
women

Needing no men to accomplish, to set in motion, to be free
Your woman isn't free, witch or no, and you know how to

Bring her to heel. A quick gulp from your flask fills you with
Righteous anger and you stride out of the shadows and
toward

The women—no, call them sluts, call them whores
Who else would dance naked under a full moon?

She still has bruises on her face from the last time you
Didn't like her actions and she reaches up, caressing them

"Come get me," she says and beckons you into the circle with
a flick
Of the fingers you always thought so elegant until you
realized she was

Nothing more than the rest of them, females to be taught a
lesson
Just like your daddy taught your mama. You grin as you cross
over

The imaginary circle these bitches think can keep them safe,
you step
One, two, three and with each foot down there's searing heat
from your toes

To your scalp. You want to scream, to make it stop, but she's
staring at you
With a look so full of hatred and power and vengeance that
you realize

This ritual, this dance, this whole goddamned thing was for
you
To catch you, to neuter you—to kill you

"I love you," you say and for you it's true: you do love her
"That's the saddest part of all of this," she says, then she
claps

Her hands near your head and you feel the fire burn the rest
of you
The bonfire has gone out because it's inside you and you
scream

As you burn, her bruises disappear. As you writhe, she watches
And does nothing, just as you did when she was the one on the ground

When First You Wooed Me

When first you wooed me, you came to me
Wearing the face of an angel
Freshly killed, stretched tightly
Held in place by samite thread
"Love me, I am good"

I would not

When next you wooed me, you came to me
With a mask of gold and copper
Citrine and apatite studded the face
Elaborate engraving adding depth and light
"Love me, I am beautiful"

I would not

When next you wooed me, you came to me
With a filigree mask of bleached wood
A dragon's visage surrounded by sacred geometry
Eyes of both day and night
"Love me, I am complex"

I would not

When last you wooed me, you came to me
With your own face, dull red and scaled
Horns growing haphazardly from your forehead
Your eyes surprisingly soft
"Love me, I am only this"

And I did

Blood in the Water

You wanted to go to the woods
When the leaves were falling around us
When the air was cool
Before the hunters but after the summer hikers

We stopped by the creek, near the rocks we visited
Once, when we first moved here
The pines and aspens around us
As you spread out the picnic you'd fixed

It was almost like old times
When love was new and we were young
And not encumbered by too much debt
And too little love

You thought I didn't know about the
Poison in the cake
You thought I wouldn't question that you
Love me, assume you'd never hurt me

You thought right
I ate it after I stabbed you
And pushed you into the creek
I ate it to celebrate my freedom

And now I'm tied here just as you are
Froth slips down my chin as blood
Darkens your shirt and you ask
"How was the cake?" without a trace of irony

I laugh because it's so you and you laugh
Because of course I stabbed you—we were
Always ones to go different routes, me with
The hands-on way out and you with the quieter option

We've been waiting for days now for a light or a door
Or even a grim reaper to show up and lead us
Wherever it is that mutual murderers go
But maybe here is the best place

Stuck with each other
Perhaps forever, perhaps only until our bodies
Are discovered by someone coming to the creek
Who knows how this works?

"Didn't think this through," you mutter
"Next time we'll coordinate better," I offer that
With a smile that may be the sweetest one
You've seen in years

You return it with one just as lovely
Who knows—maybe death will become us
Much better than life
Maybe this will be heaven, not hell

Only time will tell

The Months After the End

Rain falls, probably poisonous, maybe not
We gather it for water either way
My husband, on the porch rocking and praying
Still believes in God, in a plan, in meaning
Death and pain and this awful waiting can't faze him
Not when there's still good in the world

He means me. And his niece. He thinks we're good

We know better. There is no plan, no virtue
There's shooting first or dying
We let him sit, though, because someone
Should believe in good things
We escort strangers off our land and kill them
Goodness seeps out of us with each death

He doesn't even know they were there

The radio's gone dead three days back
We take turns listening for motors, hoofbeats, footsteps
My niece and I, ready to act—always on guard
He hums in the kitchen, milking his garden
For tomatoes and peppers and a few unwary rabbits
Cooking them on the grill like everyday barbeque

He's a person who can hold on to the past

Eventually, the past will collide with reality
Eventually someone will sneak by our defenses
Up onto his porch and try to take what's ours
And we'll slaughter whoever tries, in front of him

His wife, his brother's child, we'll die in that moment
And become what he fears most

The end of everything

We can live with that

He Sought a Dark Goddess

Tired of frills, of girlish
Giggles and silly games

He sought a darker love
In the night forest

Twisted her a crown of
Branches and dead flowers

Begged her to find him worthy
To look at him and truly

See who he was, how grim
How serious, not a trace of

Frivolity, so she looked
She pulled him apart

Inch by painful inch then
Glued him back up with a

Sticky paste made from
Obsidian and pitch and blood

As he shivered, reborn, at
Her feet, she said, "I'll pass"

I Knew

I knew, when I first met you
Those brutally green eyes
The charge of current between us
You are my home
You are my love
You are my death

Not this time, fate whispered
Or was it I who murmured for it?
The cards foretold doom
But I held on
But I held fast
But I hold my breath

Only not long enough
Head under water, your fingers in my hair
Our bath, our sacred space
Don't breathe
Don't breathe
I breathe

Breathing leads to coughing
Air out, water in
Your hands cruel on my neck
Please let go
Please let go
You don't let go

I will kill you, my last thought
As soul separates from body
Zooming past you, sodden and scratched
My love
My killer
My victim

When I come back
You'll be the weak one
For that's our pattern
I die
You die
I die, etcetera

Is the weakness in not giving up?
Or would it be weak to move on?
Find a new path, a different destiny
But you are my love
You are my life
And we'll be the death of us

Vigil

I am torn fur and
Blistered eyelids
Horrible to look at
But you never turn and see me
Not before and certainly not
Now that she's gone
I fought for her
Every rasping breath
Each sigh of pain
I would have taken
Her place if I could
But I'm only the
Monster under the bed
I could help but not heal
My skin became
Grizzled and scaled as I
Tried to make her pain
My own and sometimes
When I held my breath and
You held her hand
She knew peace
But you don't know peace
Even though you fake acceptance
For your other children
I know how much you hurt
I go under their beds now
To make sure there's no rasp
No odor of the sickness that took her
I do the best I can for them but
I don't know how to help you
How to reach someone who
Stopped believing in
Me so long ago
So I stand behind you

As you hold her picture
And weep so very quietly
That the others never wake
I'll keep the monsters
At bay—at least the
Unnatural ones like me—
While you mourn our girl

Beautiful Human

How unadvised to love me
I, an ethereal being
Of dark chiffon and spider webs
You a nondescript human with
A lopsided haircut
I was so eager to try my
Hand and you made me swear
Not to stop no matter how
Bad I turned out to be with scissors
Your good humor: such a balm
You preserve it in the face of horror

I illuminate all that is undesirable
Yet you wade through it
As though it were a feast
That never satiates
Trailing after me, laughter ringing
Making me smile even as I
Track down the ugly and the evil
"What's your favorite color?" you ask
In your never-ending attempt to know me
"Black," I say, and you laugh and laugh
Because we both know my favorite anything
Is you

Acknowledgements

"All Alone in God's House" first appeared in *Entrances and Exits*, PegLeg Publishing, ©2013

"Amateurs" first appeared in *Penumbric*, Volume V, Issue 2, ©2021

"Beautiful Human" ©2024

"Blood in the Water" ©2024

"Blood of My Blood" first appeared in *Dreams & Nightmares*, Issue 118, ©2021

"Bone China" first appeared in *Eye to the Telescope*, Issue 36, ©2020

"Caught You" first appeared in *Star*Line*, Issue 45.2, ©2022

"Close to My Heart" ©2024

"The Corvid-Human Alliance" first appeared in *Liquid Imagination*, Issue 48, ©2021

"Dark Wings" first appeared in *Burning Love & Bleeding Hearts*, Things in the Well, ©2020

"The Devil's Champion" ©2024

"Enrichment Items" first appeared in *The HWA Poetry Showcase IX*, The Horror Writers Association, ©2022

"Fetch" first appeared in *Departure Mirror*, Issue 2, ©2021

"Final Resting Place" first appeared in *Strange Horizons*, 7 March Issue, ©2022

"Good and Faithful Servant" ©2024

"He Sought a Dark Goddess" first appeared in *Kaleidotrope*, Summer Issue, ©2023

"Housemates" first appeared in *The Crypt*, May 14th Issue, ©2021

"I Knew" first appeared in *Untimely Frost - Poetry Unthawed*, Lycan Valley Press, ©2018

"I Remember This Place" ©2024

"I See You" ©2024

"A Jaunty Tune" ©2024

"Leaving the Stars Behind" ©2024

"Lost Dogs" ©2024

"Medusa Ups Her Game" first appeared in *Pyre*, Spring/Summer Issue, ©2022

"Mirror, Mirror" ©2024

"The Months After the End" first appeared in *Star*Line*, Issue 38.1, ©2015

"Pick a Card" ©2024

"Release Me" ©2024

"Slither" first appeared in *Penumbric*, Vol V, Issue 4, ©2021

"Someone Comes Knocking" first appeared in *Eccentric Orbits 3*, Dimensionfold Publishing, ©2022

"Spare the Fire, Spoil the Brute" first appeared in *The Future Fire*, Issue 52, ©2020

"Spring, When I Met You (Spring, When I Woke)" first appeared in *Dreams & Nightmares*, Issue 121, ©2022

"The Stairs" ©2024

"String Theory" first appeared in *Paper Crow,* Issue 0, ©2009

"Swamp Glow" ©2024

"Terroir" first appeared in *The HWA Poetry Showcase VI*, The Horror Writers Association, ©2019

"They Call" ©2024

"Topiary" ©2024

"Untitled in Porcelain" ©2024

"Unwilling" ©2024

"Vigil" first appeared in *Penumbric*, Vol VI, Issue 3, ©2022

"We All Want to Be Mermaids When We're Young" ©2024

"What If It Hurts?" first appeared in *Star*Line*, Issue 43.3, ©2020

"When First You Wooed Me" first appeared in *The HWA Poetry Showcase VII*, The Horror Writers Association, ©2020

"Where the Light Ends" first appeared in *Sanitarium*, Issue 4, ©2021

About the Author

Gerri Leen grew up in the Seattle area and the Olympic Peninsula but relocated to Northern Virginia in the late eighties and has never managed to leave. She's a fan of horse racing, single-origin single-harvest tea, and collecting art, especially encaustic mixed media and raku pottery.

Doused liberally in poetry at a very early age by her aunt, she nevertheless resisted doing anything other than EMO love poems until later in life. Her favorite poem is "The Second Coming" by W.B. Yeats, and the majority of her work is free verse. When she does get a hankering to work with form poetry, she enjoys creating villanelles and terzanelles, but she's fairly hopeless at sonnets. She's written one sestina and is still working off the trauma. She tends to go dark with her poetry, so horror and dark fantasy are natural landing spaces, but she also enjoys exploring fairy tales, mythology, science fiction, and more traditional fantasy. While she does have some non-genre works published, her heart tends toward the speculative.

Her poems and stories have appeared in *The Magazine of Fantasy and Science Fiction, Strange Horizons, Nature, Gamut, Dark Matter,* and the *HWA Poetry Showcase* among others. Her poetry has been nominated for the Rhysling Award, the Pushcart Prize, and the Dwarf Stars Award. She is a member of HWA and SFWA and also writes romance under the name Kim Strattford. You can find more information at her website gerrileen.com.

www.ingramcontent.com/pod-product-compliance
Lightning Source LLC
Chambersburg PA
CBHW060235180626
46813CB00007B/3090